# Chocolate Sauce and Sparkles

www.trafford.com
North America & international
toll-free: 1 888 232 4444 (USA & Canada)
fax: 812 355 4082

Printed in Canada

# Chocolate Sauce and Sparkles

E. J. MELNEY
Illustrated By: Yvonne Abuda

To the teacher who asked me this question and inspired this book.
While I am sure her name has since changed,
back then, she went by Ms. Mayoh—
a truly wonderful teacher who made a difference.

Acknowledgments:

To my mom, dad, and brother, thank you for encouraging me to write,
for telling everyone that I write, and for always believing in me.
To Ms. Kate Stevenson's grade 5 class of 2015-16 at A. Blair
McPherson school in Edmonton, Alberta, Canada.
Thank you for your amazing insights and for being
the first kids to have read this book.

Good day, my *adventurous* friends.
Thank you for picking this book.
Clearly, you are already super *awesome*.
But
I do have a very important *question* in which I need to ask you.

Do you wish to take a *journey*—nay, a *quest*—into a realm where you shall need to use your *magnificent imagination*, your *unwavering creativity*, and your delight for endless *possibilities*?

I should warn you though that this *quest* is not for the faint of heart, don't let the *butterflies* fool you.
For this quest, well *adventurous* and *epic*, shall challenge just how it is we choose to **perceive**.

But before such a *quest* can begin, a story awaits
to be told; so if it is not too bold,
"Once Upon a Time" begins what shall soon unfold.

Once upon a time, some years ago, I learned something very intriguing.
On that day, I was *overwhelmed* with feelings of *worry*,
*nervousness*, *anxiety*, *excitement*, and perhaps a bit of *fear*.
There was some of that too.

Ever felt that way before?

Well, it was on this day *facing* something which seemed *insurmountable* that I learned the most *profound* thing. For it was then that I was asked a *question*—a peculiar one, in fact, but one that would send my mind racing down a completely different *path*.

So, my adventurous *quest* takers, would you believe me if I told you that it is okay to feel *scared*, *anxious*, *worried*, *excited*, and even *nervous*? And that maybe, just maybe, those precarious *butterflies* might be a good thing after all?

If you do, then prepare yourself for a *quest* of the ages, as we shall enter a *realm* that shows you just how truly *awesome* these *butterflies* can be.

But as was said before, entering this *realm* is not easily done, for we shall first have to *venture* through some *places* not thought to be *fun*.

That is why our *quest* begins here at the edge of a *dark forest*.
The wind *howls*, the leaves *crunch*, the moon is *bright*;
there is that eerie feeling like of *Halloween night*.
Now walking through this *spooky* forest is not an easy feat.
For lit by only *moonlight*, you are guided by your *feet*.
Big *luminescent* eyes follow your every *step*, as any
slight rustle would certainly make you fret.
The *hoot* of an owl sends a *chill* down your spine, as
*worry* and *anxiety* begin to fill up your mind.
But *onward* you travel only to find a *mysterious*
door made completely of pine.

A door that opens with eerie *screeches* and *creaks* and
you find total *darkness* is all that you meet.
Immersed in such darkness, your eyes struggle to find
something that just might *quiet* your mind.

With an *outstretched* hand and a *tactful* step, *uncertain* you become of what
lies ahead. But when you take that first step, that's when you hear it—
a *bone-chilling*, *nerve-racking*, *hair-raising* sound that makes
your eyes shut tight and your feet stuck to the ground.
Then a refreshing breath of *wind* breezes upon your face
and you realize perhaps that you are in a *new* place.
For in this place, *darkness* is no longer there to greet, as you find
instead only *air* resides under those previously stuck *feet*.

You make the mistake of glancing around, and
then yes, of course, you happen to look
*down*.

For here you stand, so **high** above the ground, on a platform
that, in seconds, shall send you **hurtling** down.
Your pulse **hammers** with nervous excitement, and your heart **thumps**
inside your chest; and just when you feel the solid floor abandon
beneath your feet, you **drop** at a breathtaking, mind-bending speed.
As your eyes shut tight and a **scream** halts in your throat, you find
you land ever so slightly as though it were you could **float**.

But not before long, something *quickly* brings you *still*, as
the sound of rushing water begins to give you *chills*.
For what it is that you find is something meant to *challenge* your
mind, as a *daring* cascading rapid is what you have been assigned.

You take a moment to *observe*, only to find you
are now completely filled with **nerves**.

Although, you do happen to notice **boulders** so intriguingly spaced
in the **rapid** water which is meant to keep you in your place.
So if you haven't guessed already, then you probably already
know that **across** this **daring** rapid, you know you must go.

But such rocks are **slippery** at best and a **daring's** leap away,
with your hands and legs beginning to **shake** and your
mind **racing** with all that could go wrong.
Alas, you realize perhaps the **goal** has been to get you to **jump** all along.

From **boulder** to **land**, here you stand, in a place
they like to call no man's land.
Here in this **undesired** place is where **nerves** and **worry** begin to **overwhelm**,
where your heart **pounds**, your face **reddens**, your hands **shake**,
your mind **races**, and your stomach **flutters** as you think . . .

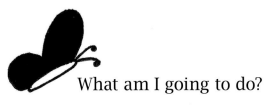
What am I going to do?

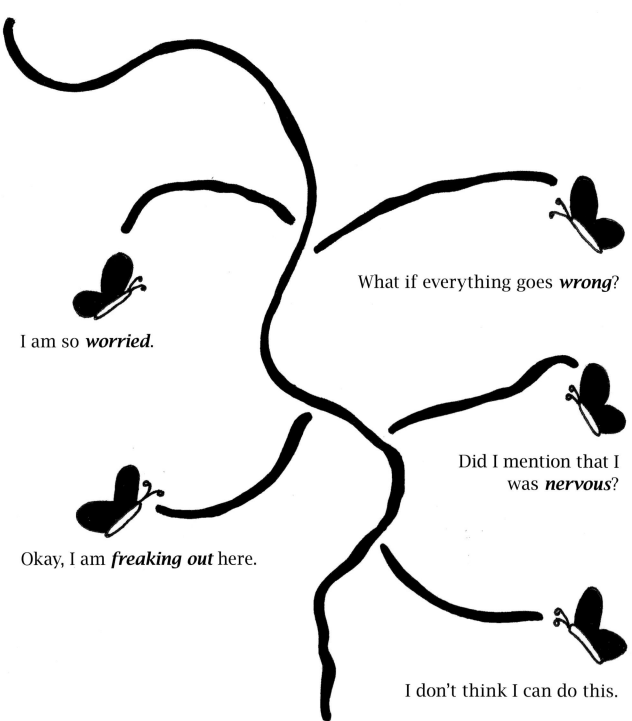

What if everything goes *wrong*?

I am so *worried*.

Did I mention that I was *nervous*?

Okay, I am *freaking out* here.

I don't think I can do this.

*But then . . .*

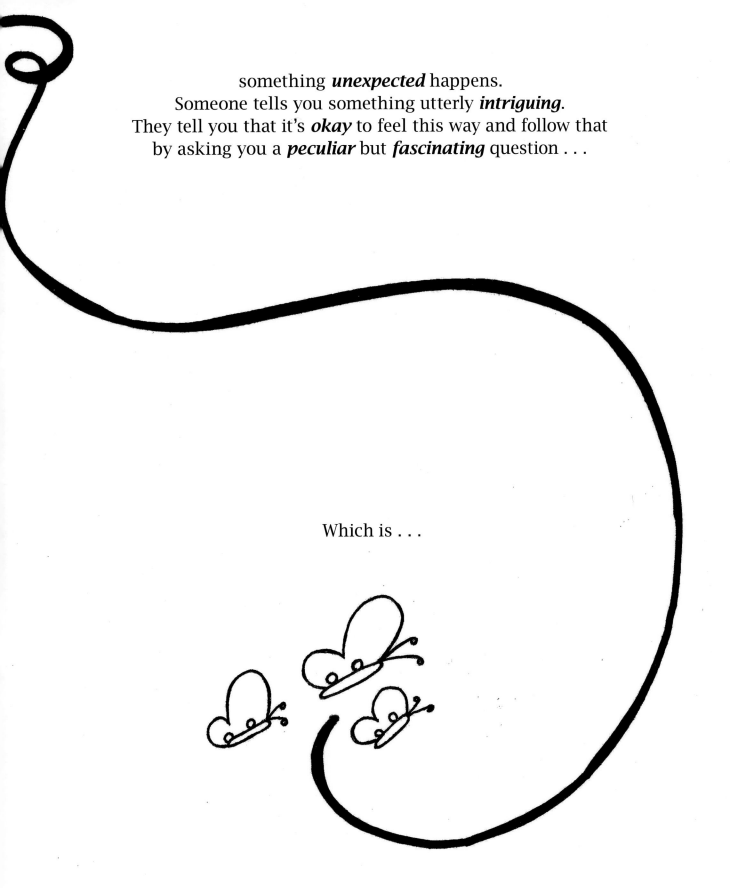

something *unexpected* happens.
Someone tells you something utterly *intriguing*.
They tell you that it's *okay* to feel this way and follow that
by asking you a *peculiar* but *fascinating* question . . .

Which is . . .

What do your *butterflies* look like?

So here we are, **quest** takers, the moment of **truth**.
Will you choose to **stay** in such a place where you can be **consumed**
by all that **worry**, **nervousness**, **fear**, **excitement**, and **anxiety**?
**Or**
will you take a **chance** and strive to understand those **heart-pounding,
nerve-racking**, and sometimes **overwhelming** feelings **differently**?

You shall find that the **choice** is yours,
as it has been all along.

But if you are indeed ready, I shall say that the
real **fun** and **adventure** awaits just ahead.
For it is there you shall find your **butterflies**
can be any kind of design.

They could be . . .

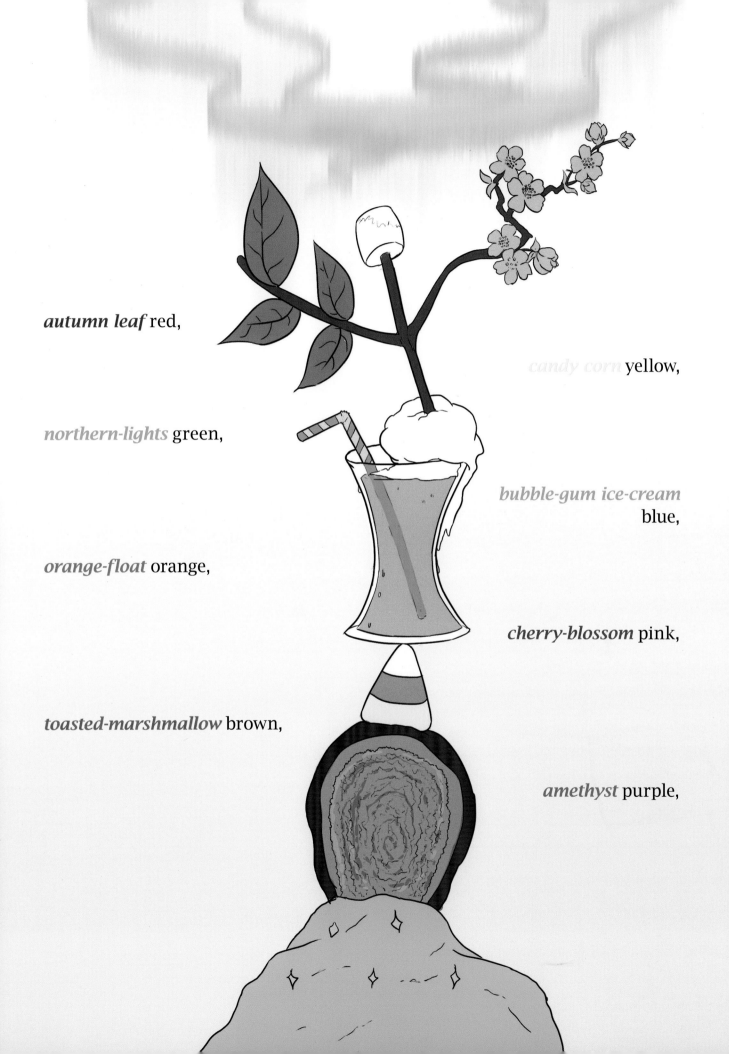

*autumn leaf* red,

*candy corn* yellow,

*northern-lights* green,

*bubble-gum ice-cream* blue,

*orange-float* orange,

*cherry-blossom* pink,

*toasted-marshmallow* brown,

*amethyst* purple,

*telephone-box* red,

*dandelion* yellow,

*key-lime* green,

*glowing-pumpkin* orange,

ocean blue,

*gumdrop* pink,

*gingerbread* brown,

or *lilac* purple.

Then again, those butterflies might just have an amazing pattern or design.
So they could be . . .

striped with **horizontal**,

*vertical,*

or **diagonal** designs;

spotted with **polka dots** that make you laugh,

or spotted like a **lady bug** or a **giraffe**.

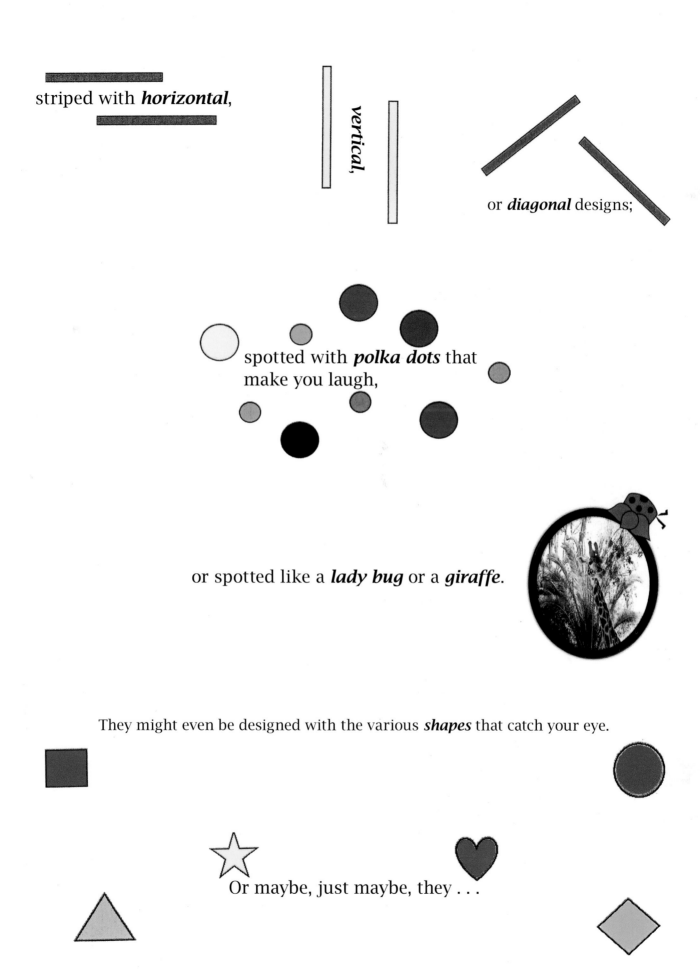

They might even be designed with the various **shapes** that catch your eye.

Or maybe, just maybe, they . . .

*glow* in the dark,

glow like a *jellyfish*,

glow like **Christmas lights** on a snowy night,

or like **flames** that crackle with light.

It is also possible that they are decorated with . . .

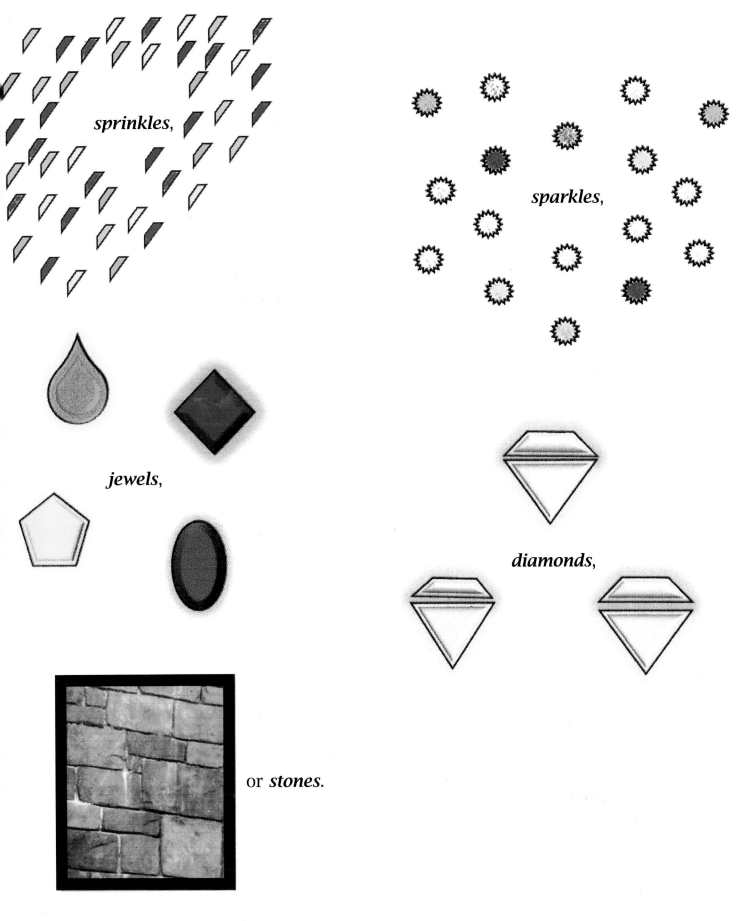

*sprinkles,*

*sparkles,*

*jewels,*

*diamonds,*

or *stones*.

Perhaps they even contain hints of *silver* and *gold*.

Or maybe those butterflies shall be . . .

the colors of a *rainbow,*

the color of
your favorite
*jelly bean,*

*neon* bright,

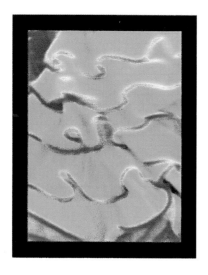

or like *fireworks* that light up the night.

Of course, those butterflies might not be just one color or design,
which shall require you to delve into your creative mind.

A mind in which those **butterflies** might be *striped, checkered, muted, or bright,* for a vastness of *possibility* lies in sight; leading one to *see* that those *fluttering* butterflies might not be such a bad thing after all, for *perspective* can be a powerful thing.

So, my dearest *quest takers*, *truth seekers*,
*creative minds*, and *adventurists* alike,
I ask you this:

*What do your*

*completely dazzling,*

*epically awesome,*

*marvelously magnificent*

*butterflies look like?*